3-16-73

The WHITE KITE

Story by RAY SIPHERD
Pictures by JUNE GOLDSBOROUGH

Bradbury Press • Scarsdale, N.Y.

The text of this book is set in 14 pt. Vladimir.
The illustrations are 3/color pre-separated wash and pencil drawings
with wash overlays, reproduced in halftone.

For Polly

Paul liked to make up stories.

One morning he saw a cat outside his window and told his parents a ferocious tiger was about to leap into the house.

Another day Paul got a pebble in his shoe and told his friends he'd found a wonderful bright diamond stolen by a gang of thieves who chased him all the way to school.

Near Paul's school was a park. One spring afternoon as he was walking home across the park he saw some children flying kites.

There were kites the shape of birds and fish and spaceships.

And kites with ribbons trailing down that danced and fluttered as they flew.

When the wind blew the kites would soar and nearly touch the clouds. Then they would swoop down and chase each other back and forth across the sky.

Paul watched the children make their kites do tricks. If he had a kite, he was sure he could make it do tricks too.

Then some boys came running toward him,
pulling on kite strings.
"Look out!" a boy called.

Paul saw a giant blue kite diving straight at him.

Whoosh! The kite whizzed past and shot into the air.

"What a big kite," Paul said to the boy.

"The biggest in the park," the boy answered, letting out more string.

"Can I fly it?" Paul asked.

"Do you know how?" the boy asked.

"Sure!" Paul said.

"Okay," the boy told him. "I'll let you fly it for a minute." He gave the string to Paul. "Now run with it."

Paul ran and the kite followed.

"Let out the string!" shouted the boy.

Paul let out the string and the kite rose higher.
Then he ran and jumped and saw the kite bounce
up and down. He waved his arm in a big circle
and the kite made a circle in the sky.

At last the boy said, "I want my kite back."

"But I can make the kite do tricks," Paul said.
"Watch!" And he waved his arm again.

"I want my kite now," said the boy.

So Paul handed him the string. The boys ran off.

The path through the park led among many old tall trees.

Paul walked along, looking up into the branches —then suddenly he stopped.

High above him in a tree was something hidden in the leaves. Paul squinted for a better look.

It was a kite string.

Quickly Paul climbed the tree, until he reached the topmost branches. There, tangled in among them, was the kite string. And it led up above the tree into the sky.

Carefully Paul untangled the string, holding it tightly so that it wouldn't get away. Then he climbed down from the tree.

He guided the string out of the tree and looked up. In the sky were kites of many colors. Paul gave his string a tug. But not one of the kites moved.

Then Paul looked above the kites.

And he saw the tiny crescent of the moon.

He pulled down on the string again....And the moon moved!

Paul blinked his eyes. He shook his head.

Then slowly he pulled down on the string once more.

The moon sank slowly.

Paul swung the kite string to the right and to the left.

The moon swung back and forth across the sky.

"I've got the moon!" Paul shouted. "My string goes up to the moon!"

When darkness came Paul hid the kite string in the tree and hurried home. He couldn't wait to tell his father and mother he had found a string that went up to the moon.

"A string that goes up to the moon?" his father laughed.

"And I can fly it like a kite!" said Paul. "When I pull down on the string, the moon dips down and when I swing it left and right, the moon swings too!"

"What a wild story!" said his father. "The moon is an enormous ball of stone thousands of miles from the earth. It could not *possibly* be on a string."

"But if it *was?*" Paul asked.

"It *isn't*," said his father firmly.

But the next day after school Paul went back to the tree in the park and untied the string and flew the moon again.

Soon he taught the moon to do tricks. When he held the string above his head and spun around, the moon spun too. When he ran and jumped and ran and jumped, the moon bounced like a piece of rubber ball across the sky.

And every day the moon grew bigger and rose higher and the string pulled harder in Paul's hand. So that he needed both hands to hold it down.

One day Paul saw some children nearby.

"See what my kite can do!" he called to them.

The children looked up at the sky. "Which kite is yours?" they asked.

"It's—the white kite," Paul said.

"I don't see any white kite," said a girl.

"And I don't," said a boy.

"You don't have a kite at all!" they shouted.

"But I *do*!" Paul told them. "My kite is the *moon*! And I can make the moon do tricks! Watch!"

He pulled on the kite string and waited.

But the moon didn't move.

Paul held the string above his head and spun around. He ran and jumped and ran and jumped again.

But the moon just sat full and heavy in the sky.

The children laughed. "Fly the moon? Make the moon do tricks? Nobody can do that!" they said, and ran off across the park.

Paul looked up at the moon and wondered. *Did* I fly the moon? *Did* I make the moon do tricks?

Suddenly the string pulled very hard against his hands. He held tight—and before he knew it he was lifted up into the air.

And when he looked down he discovered he was flying over trees and rooftops, television aerials and water towers and church spires that reached up into the sky.

Higher and higher the moon went. And faster and faster Paul let out the string to get down to the ground. Except he wasn't near the ground. And there was no more string to let out.

Paul looked down again. Below him was a pond.
If he let go of the string he would drop into
the water.

So Paul shut his eyes and held his breath and let
go. Down and down he went—and fell with a
loud *SPLASH!* into the pond.

"Paul, look at you! You're soaking wet!" his mother said as she wrapped him in a towel. "What have you been doing!"

"I was playing," Paul said.

"Playing where?" his mother asked him.

"In the park," Paul answered.

Then he stopped. He wanted to tell her about the ride the moon had given him, how he had been carried up into the sky and sailed over trees and rooftops, television aerials and water towers and tall church spires. But who would believe a story like that?

Nobody.

So Paul told his mother, "I was playing in the park...and I fell into a pond."

His mother shook her head. "I was afraid you'd tell another of those stories you made up about the moon," she said.

Paul didn't say a word.

But that night as Paul lay in his bed he thought about the moon.

He thought about the day he found the kite string in the tree.

He thought about the tricks he'd taught the moon to do.

And he thought about the ride the moon had given him that day. When slowly a light began to shine in the window of his room.

Slowly it grew brighter.

Outside in the night the moon was passing high above. Paul saw that it was very round and full and white.

And for a moment he was sure he saw a kite string trailing down below the moon as it moved across the sky.